A DAY ON SKATES

The Story of a Dutch Picnic

By

HILDA VAN STOCKUM

With Illustrations and New Introduction by the Author

BETHLEHEM BOOKS

Vancouver, Washington USA
1994

60th Anniversary edition
Original 1934 edition published by Harper and Brothers

Introduction © 1994 Hilda van Stockum-Marlin
Special features © 1994 Bethlehem Books

Newbery Medal runner-up 1935

Hardcover Edition   ISBN 1-883937-00-0

Softcover Edition   ISBN 1-883937-02-7

Library of Congress catalogue number: 93-74858

Cover art by Hilda van Stockum
Cover design by Davin Carlson

Bethlehem Books
915 W. 13th St.
Vancouver, WA 98660
Printed in the United States of America

To My Father

Who so loves children

CONTENTS

Introduction to the 60th Anniversary Edition

A DAY ON SKATES was my first book. Though I was to go on to write many more children's books, this one certainly has special memories. When Ervin Marlin, my American husband, whom I had just married, got his degree in history and political science at Trinity College, Dublin, he had to return to America to get a job. It was 1932 and America was in the depth of the Depression. Even as a wife, being a non-citizen, I would not be allowed in unless my husband had work.

So I stayed behind in Dublin, living with my mother. In order to improve our financial position I'd started on a picture book. I was a student at the school of art, so I naturally started on the pictures, making up the story as I went along. Nostalgia for my youth in Holland, and especially my experiences skating on the canals there, made me choose the subject. I was so absorbed in my task that once, having been brought a cup of tea by my mother, I accidentally dipped my brush in it while slowly sipping the paint water!

Once in America Ervin found getting a job very difficult. When Roosevelt was elected, however, he created new jobs, one of which my husband was lucky enough to get. Meanwhile he looked for a publisher for *A Day on Skates* and Harper and Brothers accepted it. They were also the publisher of the famous poet Edna St. Vincent Millay, who was related to me by marriage; she wrote the charming foreword. The book was rather a sensation at the time because of so many full-coloured pictures. It was lovely to have this asset in starting life there.

I earned money for my passage by painting portraits. As I was painting two Irish girls, Patience and Ann Conner, I told them the story of *A Day on Skates*. (I was able to borrow these portraits for my retrospective exhibition at the Royal Hibernian Academy in 1990.) The girls, who were about 9 and 11 at the time, were enchanted with the story and earnestly discussed the motives of the characters. Their enthusiasm and comments were very helpful. I'm glad of the opportunity this introduction gives to thank them both.

Hilda van Stockum

Berkhamsted, Hertfordshire
January, 1994

* *

CHAPTER I

A Skating Picnic

IN THAT small country called Holland, with its many canals and dykes, its low fields and quaint little villages, Father Frost went prowling round one January night, with his bag full of wonders. It had been a warm winter, full of rain and mist. The children had complained and the elderly people had coughed and grumbled that life was not what it used to be. How dreary that little country looked when the fields were soaked with rain and the trees stretched their naked branches hopelessly towards the gray clouds.

Nine-year-old Evert and Afke were sure that real winter would never come. Every day they had to walk to school on sleety roads, their clogs slipping along in the mud. They lived in the village of Elst, which lies in the Province of Friesland, and this January night they were fast asleep under the large thatched roof of their mother's and father's farmhouse, not knowing how busy Father Frost was outside.

First Father Frost waved his hand and snow came falling down, hushing all sound and covering everything with its downy cloak. Then he blew the clouds away, and stars began to twinkle in the dark sky. Next he blew and blew, and the rippling waters stood still and stiffened into ice. He blew and blew, and on window panes white flowers shimmered and shone. He blew, and all the raindrops trying to escape from roofs or railings froze into icicles. He blew, and the trees were clothed in silver. He blew, and the snow sparkled, twigs crackled, and people shivered in their beds. Everything he touched with his breath became magically beautiful, cold and stiff. Then the sky became rosy, and the sun, peeping out, cried, "Oh!" and all the sleepers woke up and said, "Oh!" and caught hold of their noses, which had been nipped sharply by Father Frost as he passed.

"Oh!" cried Evert and Afke. "Oh! It *is* cold."

And they pulled their bedclothes around them. They were twins, with round faces and light-blue eyes. Afke was slightly smaller than Evert and had two flaxen pigtails.

"How are we to get up?" she wailed, but Evert being a boy, was not so frightened of a little frost.

"One, two, three, hupla!" he cried. And out he was, dancing with bare feet on the cold floor, searching for his stockings.

"Look! the window is covered with ice ferns; we can't see out of it," exulted Afke. "Now we will be able to skate."

But Evert felt still more excited, for when he wanted to wash himself, he found all the water in the pitcher frozen into a lump of ice. "We'll have to manage like this," he said, smashing the lump on the floor and picking up a small piece. This he rubbed against his rosy cheek, where it soon melted and dribbled through his fingers.

Watching from her bed, Afke wanted to try it, too, and jumped out in spite of the cold. "Give me a bit," she begged, and stood rubbing it between her hands, letting the drops fall on her bare toes. Dressing that morning was a slow but interesting business, and if the twins were not so clean as usual when they went downstairs, they were at least twice as happy. In the living-room a roaring stove welcomed them with its pleasant glow. Mother stood beside it, warming a pan of milk. "Goodness!" she cried as they kissed her, "how cold you feel!"

Rushing to the window, Afke cried, "Evert, look!"

The warmth of the stove had melted the tracery of ice on the panes, and now the children could see the white and silver fairyland which Father Frost had shaken out of his bag last night. The trees in front of the house were covered with ice, looking as though they had been lifted from some giant wedding cake, and on the shimmering surface of the snow they could see no footprints except here and there the fan-shaped marking of a bird's claw.

"Now drink your milk," Mother said, "or it will get cold!"

The twins fell to, looking up only when they heard their father's footsteps in the passage.

"Good morning, everybody!" he called out pleasantly as he opened the door, bringing with him a current of cold air. "It has frozen twelve degrees in the night. We'll soon be skating," and he stooped to kiss his wife.

Afke hopped excitedly in her chair. "How soon, Father?"

"I don't know, poppet," he said, pulling her shining plait.

After breakfast Mother wrapped the children in warm mufflers, and brought them their freshly scrubbed clogs.

"I put hay inside them today," she said. "That will keep you warm and the snow will not get in."

"Give me some crumbs for the birds, Mother," begged Afke.

"I am sure they are hungry!" She got a basketful. Outside the air was clear and cold and the early morning sun seemed cold, too. Afke scattered her crumbs and watched the birds swoop down to gobble them up, pecking at each other and chattering greedily.

"They have no manners at all," she told Evert. "What would Mother say if we behaved like that?"

"Yes, just watch that big one. He gets everything," Evert cried. "Shoo!"

At last the basket was empty and it was time for the twins to leave for school. Evert walked slowly along the edge of the canal. He threw pebbles on its frozen surface, light ones which slid over it, and heavier ones which fell through. "I do hope the ice will be strong enough soon," he said. "We must hunt up our skates." Afke nodded.

Every Dutch boy and girl loves to skate, and every Dutch man and woman, too. And no wonder. Holland with its canals and streams has many miles of ice when the cold at last arrives. Both Evert and Afke had learned to skate when they were very small. Indeed, Afke had been only three when she first tottered on pigmy skates, carefully held up by her father. By now she had become quite an expert, and Evert was even better. He had won several prizes in his school's skating tournaments. One of these prizes had been a beautiful book called *Robinson Crusoe*, which he had read so often that the cover had come off. Another time he won a silver pencil, which he gave to Afke, and the last time it had been a book entitled *Good Henry*, the story of a boy who was always good. This he had promptly traded for a penknife.

"What," said Afke, dreamily, as they walked on toward school, "would you ask for if some one came and said you could have your dearest wish?"

Evert thought for a moment. "I have so many wishes, it is hard to choose. But I think I'd want the whole Zuyder Zee to be frozen up, and the North Sea, too, so that we could start out here and skate right up to the North Pole."

"That's too far," said Afke. "I'd get pain in my ankles."

"But we would take a sledge," continued Evert, "and we would tie it to the tail of a white bear. He would growl, and jump about, not knowing what was the matter with him, and then he would run and run, pulling the sledge after him. It would bump and sway over the ice, and we would hold on to each other and it would be great fun."

"Would it?" asked Afke, somewhat thoughtfully.

"Of course it would. And then we'd stay in the snow hut of some friendly Eskimo, helping him to harpoon whales."

"Hum," said Afke, "I know. You and the Eskimo would go out and leave me in the hut to clean the bones. Thank you, I hate fish, and I am not going with you. You can go by yourself."

Evert laughed. "You are a little spitfire, Afke," he said, "but I wouldn't go there without you."

They were nearing the schoolhouse now, and they could see groups of boys and girls talking excitedly. When their friends caught sight of them, they laughed and started pelting the twins with snowballs.

Suddenly the bell rang through the frosty air and the children, flushed and panting, pushed their way through the school doors. They hung their scarves and caps on numbered pegs along the walls and left their wooden shoes side by side on the floor, hastening on stockinged feet to their class-rooms. Soon the hall was deserted, its long row of clogs waiting patiently till the time when the children would return to slip them on again.

Evert and Afke were in the third form. They did not sit together, for the boys occupied the benches on the left of the room and the girls those on the right. Their class-room had a bright, freshly scrubbed appearance, as usual in Dutch schools. The benches were yellow and colored pictures hung on white-washed walls. The children looked neat, too, with well-brushed hair and clean shirts or pinafores. Their teacher was a young and cheerful person, whom they all loved. And this morning he was so pleased about the weather that he started their lessons with a song, "The White, White World." The children sang

heartily and outside on the snow-covered road many a passer-by heard them and stopped for a moment, smiling.

At the end of the day the teacher rapped on the desk for order.

"Now I have a surprise for you," he said. The children looked up eagerly.

"I have talked to the headmaster about a little plan I have and he says we may do it. It's this: If the frost continues, I am going to take all of you on a skating picnic for an entire day."

Evert and Afke and all their friends smiled in delight. A skating picnic!

"Of course you will have to ask permission of your parents," Teacher went on. "But if all is well we shall go on Friday morning."

"Hurrah!" cried the children. With a shout they hurried for their clogs. And outside they gathered excitedly into groups to talk over the coming adventure. One boy only stood by himself and seemed to hesitate. He was new and very shy. The others were too busy and happy to notice the wistful look in his eyes, so he sighed and went home alone, though he would have longed to join one of the groups. His name was Simon Smit.

* *

CHAPTER II

Evert's Accident

LUCKILY the frost continued. Every night the ice grew inches thicker, and after three days people were skating everywhere. You can imagine the excitement of Evert and Afke on Thursday afternoon. For they, as well as most of the children, had never yet been on a real skating picnic. They had often watched others start off, but now they were to have one for themselves, and it was to start the very next day.

At half-past three the school doors opened and Evert and Afke, along with their friends, hastened home. Dusk fell about them and the windows in the village houses, under their thick layer of snow, lit up here and there like twinkling eyes. The twins held hands and ran to be home sooner. Mother greeted them with a welcoming smile as they entered breathlessly. They caught the lovely smell of pea soup with pork and sausage, the favorite Dutch dish in winter-time.

"Will dinner be ready soon?" they asked.

"Six o'clock, as usual," replied Mother, "but you may have a cup of soup now if you like."

Didn't they, just! They eagerly grasped the hot cups, burning their tongues in their haste to begin.

"Greedy piglets," said Mother, smiling. "How did you like it at school today? Did Teacher say anything?"

"Mmmm," nodded Afke, swallowing a bit of sausage. "He told us to examine our skates, to take food and money with us tomorrow, and to dress warmly."

"Karel is getting a new pair of skates from his father," added Evert, "and Okke is going to be allowed to use his uncle's Frisian *doorloopers*." *Doorloopers* are skates with extra long blades on which you can go very fast.

"That's nice," said Mother, and she told them that she had already prepared the food for their journey.

"I am giving you four currant buns each, two slices of gingerbread, and also some money for hot chocolate on the way."

"Hurrah!" cried the twins, wiping their mouths. Then they went off to the smithy to have their skates sharpened. It had

grown quite dark. The snow crunched under their clogs and glittering stars appeared over their heads.

While they were still quite a way from the smithy they could see the glow from the fire, which lit up the snow on the street. And they could see little black figures moving about the light. Then they knew there were other customers who had arrived before them.

"We'll probably have to wait," said Evert.

Afke nodded. "I don't mind. The fire will keep us warm."

A crowd of boys stood around the smith's assistant, who deftly sharpened their skates one after another. Behind him the

smith himself was at work. He held a piece of white-hot iron with a pair of tongs and his little bellows boy blew the fire. As soon as the iron was hot enough the smith put it on the anvil and hammered it into shape, the sparks flying around like red stars. It was fun to watch.

Jan, the burgomaster's son, leaned against the wall so sadly that Evert went over to speak to him.

"You are coming with us tomorrow, aren't you?" he asked.

Jan sighed deeply. He was afraid not, he said. His father, who was a severe man, had taken his skates away because Jan's Christmas report had been so poor.

"I'm sorry, Jan," said Evert, when he heard his friend's story. "But perhaps he will let you come if you ask him again."

At which Jan only shook his head once more.

When the skates were ready, the twins paid their pennies and turned to go home. But Evert could not put away the thought of poor Jan. Passing the burgomaster's house, which was Jan's home, he suddenly thought of a plan. Telling Afke to wait for a moment, he climbed the front steps and resolutely rang the bell. A servant opened the door and recognized him as one of Master Jan's friends.

"He's out," she said.

"I know, but I want to see Mr. Burgomaster, please," said Evert, firmly, though he was really much frightened.

The servant looked surprised. "What might you be wanting of him?" she asked, but she let Evert in, all the same, seeing to it that he left his clogs outside. She then told him to follow her through the passage till they stood before the burgomaster's study. There she announced him by knocking hard on the door, quickly hastening away, so that when the burgomaster opened the door he saw nothing but the rosy farmer's boy, twisting his cap between his fingers.

"What's this?" he asked, not unkindly.

"I am a friend of Jan's," explained Evert, "and I came to ask . . . to ask . . ." Here his courage failed him and he traced a pattern on the floor with his stockinged foot.

"Well?"

"I . . . I . . . You see . . . tomorrow our whole class is going on a day's skating picnic with the teacher, and I thought . . . perhaps for this once you'd forgive Jan and let him come?"

The blue eyes of the boy looked coaxingly into the dark-brown eyes of the man, and they shone with such hope that the burgomaster hesitated. This was a very fine boy, indeed, and a most polite one. Besides, the burgomaster himself was a splendid skater and he knew what fun Jan would have with his friends on the skating picnic. So he twirled his mustache thoughtfully and his face softened.

"You are a good boy to think of Jan," he said. "Send my son to me. I believe that for this once I shall forgive him, but I must talk to him myself."

Evert grinned with delight, gripping the burgomaster's hand. "Thank you, sir, thank you!" And off he hurried to tell Jan the good news. Outside the door he slipped on his clogs and, pulling Afke after him, he shouted, loudly, "Jan! Oho! Oe! Ja-a-a-n!"

Jan came slowly out from the smithy door.

"Jan, you're to go to your father," Evert called, happily. "He says you can have your skates."

As soon as Jan heard the news, he ran for home as fast as he could go.

"I would have hated to leave him behind," said Evert.

"I would, too," said Afke, "but now it is your turn to carry the skates. I'm frozen." And all the way home she blew on her fingers.

The next morning the twins were awakened early by their

mother, who gave them their breakfast and dressed them in warm sweaters and shawls. They wore their Sunday boots, too, for only very clever people can skate in clogs. Then they set out, their skates dangling and clanking on the orange straps in their hands.

The village was still dark, but there was a glimmer of light on the horizon. In the cold air their breaths came out like smoke and they puffed and blew to make a big cloud of it. As soon as they came near to the school, they saw that Teacher was already there, with many of the boys and girls around him. He carried a gaily colored pole with which he threatened the girls, who rushed out of his reach with shrieks and giggles. He was dressed in a sweater, with a woollen cap to match.

"Are we all here?" he asked, after waiting for another few minutes. Evert looked around and saw Okke wearing his scarlet shirt. Jan stood next to Okke, his eyes shining with happiness, and Simon was on the other side, by himself, as usual. How queer Simon was, never playing games with the rest, always so cross if you spoke to him. Evert himself was naturally a friendly boy and he could not understand why anyone should be as shy as Simon.

Now Teacher looked over his boys and girls. "All here. Well then, we'll go."

So off they went, marching along the road past the big windmill, its skeleton wings dripping with icicles, on to the canal, where they put on their skates.

Afke had some difficulty in fastening hers, for they were a bit small for her, and the straps had seen better days. Suddenly she pulled so hard that one came off, and she fell over backward into the snow, with her legs in the air. Everyone laughed merrily at this, and Teacher, who rushed to pick her up, said, "Are you trying to go to bed in the snow, Afke? It's a nice clean bed, but rather cold."

"No," Afke replied, with a twinkle in her eye, "I wasn't trying to go to bed, but I was resting my feet a bit."

"We'll rest later," Teacher told her, smiling. "Wait till you have skated some twenty miles." He fixed the strap for her, and the others having tied on their skates and tested them, all were ready to start. Teacher gripped the front of the long pole, inviting the seven girls to hang on to it behind him, while Okke brought up the rear. The rest of the boys skated alone or in

couples, laughing at the girls who made such a prim and pretty picture as they sailed along demurely in a row.

Afke felt a bit wobbly at first and she was glad to have the support of the pole and the aid of the teacher's vigorous strokes.

She was frightened, too, of the cracks and bumps in the ice. What if her skate got caught in one? Then she would fall! That would be horrid. She fixed her eyes timidly on her feet, catching her breath every time she traveled over a lump.

Evert noticed this and called out to her: "Head up, silly. Don't look down or you will be sure to stumble. There, that's the girl." For Afke had lifted her face, and soon she forgot her fear in looking at the fine scenery around her. It was fun, too, to skate along keeping time with the others in her strokes.

Now they pushed forward swiftly along the glittering canal and were soon surrounded by white fields, with a few bare trees here and there making a lovely picture against the sky.

The morning haze parted and the sun rose. The skaters **watched** it breathlessly, listening to the barking of a dog, the long-drawn-out crowing of a cock.

"Oh!" said Afke, gazing at the upward flight of two starlings, "I wish *I* had wings!"

"You'll get them some day," said Okke, "if you are good."

Now Teacher started a song, *Ik wou dat ik een vogel was,* or, in English, "I wish I were a bird," and the children joined in, their voices chiming prettily in the frosty air.

"Isn't it great!" thought Evert. "Isn't it all beautiful!" His wide blue eyes missed nothing. They wandered from sturdy little Afke to lanky Okke and to Jan's slight figure. "We've still got the whole day before us," he thought, with a sigh of content, "and everybody is happy."

Now he skated toward Jan, on whose shoulder he laid a friendly hand. "I'm glad you could come, Janneman!"

Jan looked up grate-fully. "Thanks to you, my friend," he said. "Just fancy missing all this," and he took a deep breath, catching hold of Evert's hand for a sprint. Off they went as quick as the wind, the others watching them with ad-miration. Okke watched so well that he paid no attention to his balance,

and when his skate struck a wisp of straw he fell down with a bang, dragging several girls on top of him. The others were saved by Teacher, who swerved sharply to the left with the pole, pulling the line of girls around like a tail. They laughed heartily, for no one was hurt. Okke remarked that the ice, at

any rate, felt a good deal softer than Siepertje's elbow, which had just hit him in the stomach, and the girls teased him as they slapped the snow from their skirts, telling him that he had been put behind to protect them and not to pull them down!

"Come along," cried Teacher. "We can't waste too much time." So they continued their journey and soon came to a draw-bridge underneath which they had to pass. This wasn't easy, for the bridge was low and they must crawl on all fours, even

Teacher! Afke pretended she was a lame duck, and made many funny noises.

"You'd better stop that," said her brother, "or some one will catch you and roast you for dinner!" a remark that sent Afke off into peals of laughter.

They were glad when they left the cold shade of the bridge and were out in the warm sunshine again with a beautiful stretch of ice before them.

A path had been cleared by the *baanveger*, the ice-sweeper, an old man with unshaven chin and a big broom in his hands. They called out to him and gave him some pennies. *"Dank je wel,"* he said, touching his cap.

As time went on more and more people came out on the ice, and here and there tents were being erected. Some of these tents had benches in front of them on which tired skaters could rest. There was also the smell of delicious hot cocoa and wafers, with one man calling from a tent door:

> "Hot milk and cold cake:
> Sit down to partake."

"Yes, yes, let's," cried Afke. She was hungry, and besides her legs were getting shaky. Some of the boys and girls now complained that their skates were coming loose, so Teacher picked out a nice clean-looking tent and ordered them all to stop. This they did gladly, with a great scraping of skates, and falling onto the wooden benches, they looked at the food on the table with hungry eyes. A fat lady served them, smiling good-naturedly as she lifted the lid from a kettle of steaming cocoa. Everyone got

a big cupful and a *korstje*, which is a little spicy Dutch cake, especially beloved by skaters. They munched, and warmed their hands on the hot cups, while Teacher lit his pipe and puffed away.

Evert settled himself contentedly. It was so jolly to be tired and hungry and then to sit down and let hot chocolate trickle down your throat. He nodded and winked at Afke, who nodded back so vigorously she choked on a *korstje* and had to be slapped on the back till she'd coughed up the crumb.

By now they had finished their food and were sitting watching the many skaters on the ice—beginners struggling behind chairs, schoolboys who skated swiftly, and many fat women who puffed as they did their best. And Evert and Afke and their friends couldn't help but laugh when every now and then some one would come down with a thud.

Then Teacher rose; it was time to be moving. So once more the children tied on their skates firmly and were ready for further adventures.

After they had been skating along for ten minutes or so, they saw a large crowd of people gathered around an artist who sat in front of his easel, painting the view. He was well protected against the cold, wrapped in a fur coat with a cap drawn firmly over his ears, so that only a beard and frost-bitten nose could be seen.

"Let's have a look," suggested Evert, who loved to paint and draw, himself, and who was therefore greatly thrilled to see a real artist at work. Teacher felt as curious as his class; so they joined the crowd. The picture the artist was painting was a splendid representation of a winter scene in Holland. And he was making it all so real that the children cried with delight when they saw it. They especially admired the little skaters in the picture, wearing their red and yellow petticoats or blue pants, and they liked the sledges, the tents, the horses, and the dogs. All were delicately painted against a background of white fields, and at the back was a little Dutch village with its slender steeples rising above the snowy roofs.

The children pushed forward, following the artist's movements with great interest, eager to learn as much as they could.

They saw him dipping his brush in a bottle of turpentine and wiping it with a dirty rag. Then he pushed it in one of the little blobs of color on his palette, mixing another color with it and softening the mixture with white till it was of the right shade. He looked at his canvas with his head on one side and his eyes all screwed up, very carefully adding some tiny spot of color to his picture. Then he leaned back, holding his brush in the air and peeping through half-closed eyes.

Next he frowned and said, distinctly, *"Wat bliksem!"*, which is a Dutch swear word which I am not going to translate for you. The tiny spot of color, which one could scarcely see, must have been a mistake for he quickly started scraping it off with his palette knife, dropping his rag to the ice as he did so. Evert quickly picked it up for him.

"If you please, sir, you dropped this!"

The artist raised his head. "Thank you," he said, interested at once in Evert's eager face.

"That's a lovely picture, sir. Just the way things look on a day like this." The artist smiled, pushing back his cap and giving the children a glimpse of his friendly blue eyes.

"You like it, eh?" he said.

Evert nodded. "I wish I could paint like that," he said. "I draw sometimes, chickens and pigs, but this is much more difficult, isn't it?"

"Indeed it is!" said the artist, going back to his work.

"Do you use no water?" inquired Evert, who had never seen anyone paint in just this way before.

The artist took a brush from his mouth. "No. In oil painting you mix with oil."

Teacher drew near. "Do you ever exhibit in Leeuwarden?" he asked. Leeuwarden is the capital of Friesland, and many artists show their work there.

The artist nodded. "I had a big landscape in last year's gallery," he said. "My name is Van der Velde."

"Oh!" exclaimed Teacher in an awestruck voice. "Yes, indeed. Your picture was one of the most beautiful there. 'Meadows in Springtime'—I remember it well."

"Nonsense!" protested the artist, modestly. "It was not half so good a picture as some others of mine. It just happened to please people."

Teacher didn't know what to say to this, so he changed the subject. "We've several young artists in our class," he went on. "Here is one of the best of them," and he put his hands on Evert's head. "Yes, this boy has a real talent and will perhaps become an artist like you one day."

The artist turned toward Evert and smiled. "What is your name, sonny?" he inquired.

"Evert Jansen."

"Well, I'll look out to see your name some day in the Ryksmuseum."

The children laughed and came still closer to watch the

artist. But Teacher soon said that it was time to leave him to his work. So they continued their journey.

After skating another quarter of an hour or so, they left the canal for a frozen stream which would lead them to the town of Snaek. This stream was more interesting to follow, as it wound its way between fields and shrubberies, bringing new things to see every minute. But the ice was not good here. Along the side there were air-holes and cracks, and every so often squares had been cut in the ice, where the people of the neighborhood came to fish for eels.

It was now nearly noon. The willow trees on either bank shone golden in the sunlight, letting the blue sky peep through their branches, and the only sounds to be heard were the crunching of the skates and the twittering of hungry birds. The twins specially noticed the *cheep-cheep* of the wren which is called Winterkoninkje (little winter king) in Holland.

Evert skated in front of the others, enjoying it hugely. He liked to imagine himself an explorer going into unknown regions and finding things that no one ever found before. When the river curved, hiding itself behind willow trees and hazel bushes, he pretended that wolves were waiting behind the bend, licking their chops and thirsting for his blood. He skated cautiously, in order to be able to defend himself at any moment against their greedy onslaught, and he was very sure he would conquer them, take off their skins, and return home a hero. But when he passed the corner there were no wild beasts. Nothing was there before him but a glittering ribbon of ice winding itself between snow-covered fields and inviting him to breathe deeply and to go on as fast as his legs would carry him.

Above his head a flock of pigeons circled on sunlit wings against the brilliant sky. It was all so beautiful and Evert felt himself gliding more swiftly, the wind singing in his ears and trees flashing past him. The clear air seemed to draw him up toward the sky. "Hurrah!" he cried.

Suddenly he stumbled on a rough bit of ice and fell, slithering along straight toward a fishing-hole. Simon, who had also been skating by himself not far away, too shy to join in the others' fun, saw his danger and gave a scream, but it was too late. There was a tremendous cracking of ice, a splashing of water, and Evert fell right into the dangerous spot.

* *

CHAPTER III

Snow Pancakes

SIMON turned deadly pale. He saw Evert splashing about, frantically crying for help and trying to find support on the edges of the broken ice, which only crumbled farther as he caught at them. For a moment Simon did not know what to do. Then he stretched out on the ice and slowly crawled toward the hole, taking care not to press heavily on any particular spot lest the ice might crack again. When he was near enough, he stretched out his arms and Evert gratefully grasped them, hanging on to them for dear life, his teeth chattering with the cold.

"Help! Help!" they both cried.

But already Teacher's welcome voice rang in their ears. "Hold on, Simon. I'm coming!" And calling to Jan and Okke to run quickly for help to the house across the field, Teacher held out the long pole to Evert and Simon. Simon freed one arm to grasp the end. Then, with all the boys of the class helping, poor Evert was pulled from the water.

Meanwhile Jan and Okke had been to the farmhouse, where the farmer's wife had given them warm blankets. These were wrapped around Evert as soon as he struggled on land. Everyone took off his own skates and helped Teacher take Evert as quickly as possible across the snowy fields to the farm.

Afke's legs were short. She was soon left trudging along sadly with Simon, who had also fallen back of the rest. Evert's accident had frightened her. She still felt her heart thumping.

What if her dear twin brother had been drowned? "Oh!" she exclaimed, clasping her hands, "I'm *glad* he's saved! Thank you, Simon, oh, thank you!"

When they approached the house Mrs. Sjollema, the farmer's wife, came rushing out to meet them. She was very sorry for Evert, exclaiming, *"Och die arme Jongen!"*, which means, "Oh, that poor boy!"

"He must be warmed up immediately," she said. "I've laid hot bottles in our bedstead and he can crawl in there while I hunt for dry clothes. Come in, all of you!" And she bustled off with Evert, leaving the others to follow as they pleased.

saying to Mrs. Sjollema that to have such a crowd for lunch would be far too much work for her.

"Nonsense!" said she. "It's a treat for me to have visitors. We see very few people. No, it's no use objecting. I'll simply be insulted if you leave."

Teacher saw that it was impossible to resist so hospitable and enthusiastic a hostess. "Well, I'm much obliged to you," he said, and added to the cheering children, "Now, be quiet and behave yourselves at your very best so that Mrs. Sjollema does not need to regret her kindness. Perhaps we can help her with something to show our gratitude."

"I can lay the table," piped Siepertje.

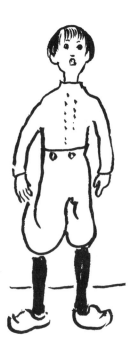

Teacher sighed with relief. He had been anxious about Evert, but now he felt sure all would be well. They entered the spacious, cheerful kitchen, full of shining brass ornaments and copper pots and pans, and immediately hurried over to the stove, where a huge fire burned. Mrs. Sjollema soon came back with Evert's dripping garments and hung them up to dry. She nodded to the children and said, smiling: "He's asleep already, poor boy. He was so tired. Just you wait and in an hour he'll be as right as rain!"

"It is very good of you to take such trouble about him," said Teacher, gratefully. "Come, children, we'll go out to eat our lunch and then return for Evert."

"No such thing," said Mrs. Sjollema, cordially. "You are all going to stay for lunch and I'll fry some snow pancakes."

"Hurrah!" cried the children. But Teacher silenced them,

"And I can wash up," added Afke.

"But what are we to do?" asked the boys.

Mrs. Sjollema laughed. "The girls may stay here to help me, but you boys had better go out and enjoy yourselves. Oh, here is my son! He'll show you round the place." For a boy about ten years old had entered the kitchen and stood staring with amazement at all the strangers.

"Tjerk," said his mother, "this is a gentleman from Elst and he is on a skating picnic with his class. One little boy fell through the ice and nearly drowned, but they rescued him and now he is sleeping upstairs. They are all staying for lunch, so you had better show them the farm." Tjerk appeared staggered by so much news and regarded the children with open mouth.

"Can't we do anything for you?" asked Teacher, addressing Mrs. Sjollema. "Here we are," he added, smiling, "a lot of strong men out of work. Surely you have some job for us."

Mrs. Sjollema thought for a moment. "Yes, I have," she

admitted. "I have been asking my husband for several days to clear away the snow in the yard, but he has been too busy . . . so if you like . . ."

"Of course! The very thing!" cried Teacher. "Come, boys, we'll start at once." And off they went, Tjerk showing them the way and giving them spades and coal-shovels with which to work.

Mrs. Sjollema watched them with a smile, then returned to her kitchen to prepare batter for the pancakes. The girls flitted about the room, laying the table and fetching spoons and bowls. "Now I must have some nice clean snow," she said.

"Who'll go and get it?" Afke and Siepertje volunteered, so they were sent off with a large pan.

"Brrrr! How cold it is outside after the warm kitchen!" exclaimed Siepertje. "Let's quickly scratch away the dirty snow and fill the pan with beautiful clean stuff underneath, so that the pancakes will be nice."

But Afke was in no hurry. She was staring at the boys, who were struggling with shovelfuls of snow, while Teacher shouted directions. They looked busy and happy and had already cleared a large space, piling up the snow at the back of the yard.

Siepertje filled her pan and tugged at Afke's sleeve, "Come, Mrs. Sjollema is waiting."

The kitchen was soon filled with the smell of fried pancakes, and the boys came trooping into the room, gladly sniffing up the smell, for they felt hungry. The girls greeted them with excited exclamations. "Look, we've all laid the table. And you never saw the cakes being made, it was such fun watching. Mrs. Sjollema flipped them into the air and caught them back in her pan with the other side up."

"And they are real snow pancakes. I saw her mixing the snow with the flour."

Mrs. Sjollema now disappeared, and came back a moment later with Evert dressed in a suit of Tjerk's which quite fitted him. He looked rosy and happy and laughed when the boys cheered him.

"Don't cheer me. Cheer Simon," he said. And shy Simon smiled happily at the rousing cheers. Then Mrs. Sjollema told the teacher that Evert's clothes would not be dry for some time, but that her husband could bring them in his car and take back her son's suit.

"That's very, very kind of you," Teacher exclaimed. "I'm most grateful."

"Hullo! What's all this?" a deep voice boomed from the doorway.

"There's my husband!" cried Mrs. Sjollema, and hurried to explain the presence of the guests. Mr. Sjollema proved to be a big burly farmer with a square, good-humored face. He was amused with his visitors and at once started teasing the girls, threatening them with all sorts of dreadful things if the pancakes weren't a success.

"We do have a large company for lunch today," Mrs. Sjollema said, laughing, "but we'd better begin or the pancakes will get cold."

As many as could now took seats around the table. But they didn't all fit and some of the children had to find places on turned-up baskets or footstools. There was a rustling of paper while they unpacked their sandwiches, which had gotten rather squashed in the journey. The pancakes certainly looked much more appetizing. Each boy and girl was happy to have a big, round, steaming one, with heaps of sugar on top.

Mr. Sjollema wanted to hear about the skating picnic and Afke, who sat near him, gave him a complete account of all their adventures, illustrating her narrative with a fork at the end of which a piece of pancake dangled. A particularly violent gesture loosened the morsel from the fork and it flew over the table, hitting Mr. Sjollema on the nose. They all laughed merrily over this, especially as Afke herself looked so disgraced. Tjerk

comforted her by putting a second pancake on her plate, which, as Evert remarked, was going to make her rounder than she was already.

After lunch the girls helped Mrs. Sjollema to wash up, and then Teacher said it was time to start again, as they had still a long way to go. At his words, Tjerk went over to him and asked whether he might go with the class to Snaek, where he had to do an errand for his mother.

"Indeed, yes!" agreed Teacher. "You are quite welcome. I cannot thank Mrs. Sjollema enough for all her kindness."

So they took a cordial farewell of the farmer and his wife and started off, Mrs. Sjollema waving good-by to them from the doorstep.

* *

CHAPTER IV

Evert's Plan

AS SOON as they were back on the ice again, Tjerk took the pole and offered to pull the girls. They accepted rather timidly, for none of them was anxious for more accidents. But Tjerk soon proved to be a very good skater, guiding them carefully past dangerous places.

When tying on his skates Evert whispered something to Jan and Okke, and the three stayed behind, following the rest of their class at a distance. They wanted to talk by themselves, for Evert had promised his friends to tell them a secret. And none of them, not even Evert, thought to ask Simon to share their plans, and he was too shy to force himself on them.

"What is it?" asked Jan and Okke as soon as the others were out of earshot.

"I shall tell you, but you must not let anyone know about it. That would spoil the fun," Evert said, mysteriously. "It came to me while I was in bed and it seemed a fine scheme. You know that book I got last year, *Robinson Crusoe,* eh?"

"Yes," the others cried. "You lent it to us."

"Well, I was just thinking what a pity it is that we've no desert islands near Holland where we could go and have adventures. I'd like to be Robinson Crusoe. Wouldn't you?"

His friends agreed.

"Why shouldn't we pretend we are? Couldn't we practise being explorers, and be real ones later on? Couldn't the three of us form a club and have some hut in a lonely place that nobody knows of?" The other boys looked at him with eager faces.

"It seems great, but how are we going to manage it?" asked Jan, who felt doubtful, because they looked after him so well at home that he was afraid any exploring on which he might venture would be immediately discovered.

Evert scratched his head. "There are difficulties, of course," he admitted. "For instance, I don't think we can find a really secret spot anywhere around Elst. But I know of something nearly as good. We have a patch of arid land at the back of our farm where heaps of nettles grow and low shrubs."

"Oh, I've seen it," said Okke. "Didn't we play hide and seek there on your last birthday party?"

Evert nodded and continued: "I asked Father whether we could use it for our games, and he said I might because it wasn't good soil. It is not a very large place, but big enough to explore in. We could always imagine that we were on an island, which would make it more exciting."

"Yes, but what if other people come messing around?" inquired Okke.

"I'll ask my father to put up some wire so that we can have it to ourselves and then we can build a hut there and make our own things. For we must not have any help from home. We must make everything ourselves just as though we were really stranded."

"Could we sleep in there sometimes?" Jan asked. "That would be fun."

"I am sure my mother wouldn't mind," said Evert, "but I don't know about your people."

"No," muttered Jan, dejectedly, "I don't either. I fear the worst."

"Never mind. We'll have meals there, anyway. We'll cook potatoes on a fire and eat them with our fingers. We must each have a suit of old clothes so that we can do anything without being scolded afterward. Besides, old clothes will make it more real."

"Couldn't we be pirates instead of explorers?" Okke asked,

who had just been reading a book called *Under the Black Flag*, which was very thrilling.

Evert, however, thought that a childish plan. "No one can become a pirate nowadays," he said. "That used to be all right,

but people are put into prison for it now, while you can be an explorer even today. Teacher says that there are large parts of the earth quite undiscovered."

The others nodded hastily, and Okke said: "Of course I see the idea. We are to be something real, not just something imaginary. We must prepare ourselves for later. That's a good idea."

"If only my mother wasn't so difficult about these matters," sighed Jan.

"Well, you can do other things," said his friends, consoling him. "But what are we going to call ourselves?" They thought for some time and then Jan, who had read more than the others, suggested "The Three Columbians," after Columbus, who discovered America.

"Perhaps later on we'll find some world even bigger than America," he said, hopefully. "It's a pity Columbus did not hit on something else, leaving America for us, then we could have had exciting times with red Indians."

So the three talked on and on, delighted with their scheme and suggesting more improvements.

In the meantime the others skated swiftly along, admiring the changing scenery, for the river turned and twisted in a picturesque way, leading them past farms, through brushwood or underneath the overhanging branches of dark trees. Suddenly, after a sharp bend, it opened out into a wide lake, drawing a cry of delight from the children, "Oh, how lovely!"

A vast expanse of glittering ice held their enchanted gaze. Nothing but ice as far as they could see, with the blue sky coming to meet it at the horizon, and against the sky in the distance two windmills and the faint gray marks of reeds and rushes bordering the lake. On the ice were many little figures darting to and fro or clustering around tents from which flags were flying merrily. Strains of music from a band drifted toward them on the breeze. "How jolly!" cried the children, looking at Teacher with shining eyes.

Teacher smiled and counted his sheep. "We must wait till we are all together before going any farther," he said, "or some of us might get lost in the crowd. Where's Evert?"

"He's coming behind us with Okke and Jan," Simon informed him, looking back. "They'll soon be here."

The children fidgeted. Impatient to try the smooth ice of the lake, they were glad when the three loiterers caught up with them at last.

Teacher proposed that they should take each other by the hand and skate side by side to make full use of the fine stretch of ice. So they joined up, forming a long line and singing the Dutch national anthem, "Wilhelmus van Nassaue," as they went.

They skated so fast that Afke could not keep up with their strokes and had to let herself be dragged along, which was certainly much easier.

Suddenly Teacher slowed up and cried out: "Wait a minute. I believe I see a friend of mine." And he hastened toward a young man who was performing a beautiful circle with one leg in the air. "Hullo, Arie!" The young man stood abruptly on his feet again and gladly thrust out his hand.

"Gerard!" he exclaimed. "Of all people! What are you doing here? I'd thought you'd be at school."

"No," smilingly explained Teacher. "We are on a skating picnic, the children and I. This is the lot. We are going on to Snaek, and from there we'll take the short cut home. We have had heaps of adventures. Haven't we, children?"

The children, who had been looking shyly at the new arrival, nodded and smiled.

"This is delightful," cried the young man whom Teacher addressed as Arie. "If you don't mind, I'll go with you a part of the way. Have the children been to the *poffertjeskraam* yet? No? That's a shame! Then come along and I'll treat you!" He took the pole, dragging as many of the children with him as would come, the others following breathlessly.

One of the tents sold *poffertjes*, tiny round cakes made of flour and milk, whose delicious fragrance now greeted them. A man in a white apron stood before a stove in the tent and was busily frying, for there were crowds of boys and girls in front, all there to buy *poffertjes* for their pennies.

Teacher and his friend settled themselves on a bench and talked about old times, leaving the children to feast on plates full of hot *poffertjes* served with butter and sugar.

Simon leaned against the tent pole and watched the throngs and throngs of skaters pass, all dressed so differently, and yet from a distance so alike. He felt somewhat lonely and looked longingly over to where the Three Columbians were eating from one plate, to practise economy.

"Evert's never alone; always with Okke and Jan. I wish I had chums like that," and he sighed deeply, trying to picture to himself the delights of friendship. For he had been an orphan for as long as he could remember and had lived on a lonely farm with a sour old aunt for the greater part of his life till he came to Elst, to live with an uncle who was not able to understand why his nephew was so lonesome. So he had never known what it was to have boys to play with. In fact, he did not know how to play with them. Whenever he was with Okke and Jan and Evert, he could think of nothing at all to say. So, too, when he was with the others. He just stood there, looking at them. No wonder the Elst children thought him queer!

Afke had now finished her *poffertjes* and looked up. "There is Simon, doing nothing," she thought. "He looks unhappy. And if it hadn't been for him, Evert might have been drowned." Going over to his side, she joined him in admiring the gay scene in front of them and smiling over the movements of feeble skaters. They laughed together again and again, until all Simon's loneliness vanished and his brown eyes sparkled.

The other children had by now emptied their plates and were licking their sticky fingers. "What is the time?" Teacher asked, hastily consulting his watch. "Half-past two! Dear me! then we must be getting on!"

"I'm going to bring you to Snaek," said Mr. Arie De Wit, for that was his full name, producing a mouth organ and starting to play a gay tune.

"That's right, be our band," said Teacher, with a laugh. "Come, boys!"

It took them some time to cross the lake. Then they turned into a straight canal which would bring them to the little town. After the perfect surface of the lake, the ice here disappointed them, for it was full of yellow spots and cracks.

They now had to proceed carefully, Evert and his two friends skating in front. "We can pretend," he whispered to the others, "that we are chief explorers on a North Pole expedition and behind us is the crew." This was a great game which amused them very much. To the right and to the left they now and again passed gay little houses made of red brick or wood painted green.

"Those are the huts of Eskimos," explained Evert. When they passed some barges lying dark and motionless in their prison of frozen water he whispered, "Those are whales," causing Okke and Jan to explode in spluttering laughter. The children behind noticed this with curiosity, and Afke thought: "They are having a secret together. Never mind. Evert is sure to tell me about it later." For the twins shared everything.

CHAPTER V

More Adventures

IT WAS fascinating to go into the town by the canal. Up above, the people looked like mechanical dolls, and the street cars like playthings. It seemed, too, that no one saw them at all, and that soon they could shout, "Surprise!" and everyone would be astonished.

Very quietly the teacher and his boys and girls now made their way through the famous watergate into the city of Snaek. The children had seldom been outside Elst, for their parents were busy folk who did not have time to take their sons and daughters with them when they went marketing. So to Evert and Afke and their friends this skating picnic was a magic journey and what they now saw seemed part of fairyland. Indeed, they were so much taken up by the sights around them that it was a wonder no more accidents happened. They paid so little attention to their feet.

The canal narrowed considerably after it passed under the watergate and circled round the center of the town. From where they were down below on the canal the children could plainly see the streets at either side. They saw salesmen walking behind their carriages and hoarsely shouting their wares. They saw women with shawls wrapped round them, chatting with their neighbors, children building up a snowman or fighting with each other, and last but not least they spied a huge barrel organ, which by its merry jingle had attracted crowds of boys and girls, who were dancing joyfully around it.

When our skaters passed the marketplace, they stopped. "Let's get off here," Teacher suggested, "and explore the city."

The marketplace, so full of buyers and sellers in the morning, now looked deserted except for some men who were packing up the remains of Friday's cheese market. At the opposite side of the square stood a beautiful old church with a high tower which tapered off to a point on which a golden weather-cock glittered in the sunshine.

"That's a great building," said Mr. De Wit, who had taken off his skates and was walking toward it. "It dates from the fifteenth century."

Afke looked up, but shut her eyes immediately. "It makes

one dizzy, it's too high," she cried, for she had never before seen anything taller than a poplar tree.

Evert was full of admiration and he tugged at Teacher's elbow, "Please sir, was the tower Michiel de Ruyter climbed as high?" Teacher smiled and nodded.

All Dutch children love the story of their famous admiral, Michiel de Ruyter, who lived in the time of William III of Orange. And they like to hear how the great man was a mischievous boy in his youth, who got chased away from school and had to turn a ropemaker's wheel for a living. One day, so the story goes, he escaped and climbed the tower in Flushing, the little town where he lived. He climbed right up on the steeple, kicking off slates from the roof to find support. At last he reached the enormous weather-cock, to which he held fast, looking far over the roofs to the wide, wide ocean beyond, where ships sailed to distant countries and where his heart was drawn. But he had to climb down again when his hunger warned him that it was time for dinner. When he reached the ground he found the marketplace in a turmoil. Several old women had nearly fainted with terror, and every one was indignant with the reckless boy. He got a sound beating from both his father and his master for having wasted his time, spoiled the roof of the steeple, and risked his life. This, of course, is a warning to any one who might feel inclined to try similar tricks, but it is comforting to think that Michiel de Ruyter became one of Holland's great admirals, winning his fame on that very sea which he had admired from the steeple.

Teacher and his class now walked through the quaint and narrow streets of the little town. The children looked eagerly at the shop windows, the girls pointing out pretty scarves, the boys more intent on footballs and popguns.

Tjerk did his errand, which was to deliver a note to the proprietor of a dairy shop, and the others waited outside for him.

A small boy at the corner of the street was crying and rubbing his eyes with grubby hands. Afke, who couldn't see tears without wishing to help, went up to him. "What is the matter?" she asked, stooping to look at his little face.

"I lost my penny in the snow," the child sobbed, "a beautiful new penny." Mr. De Wit, who had followed Afke, at once took a penny from his pocket and handed it to the small boy, expecting a bright smile. The child took it, looked at it silently for a moment, and then burst forth into a fresh wail.

"Why," said Afke, "now you have your penny, why don't you cheer up?"

"Yes," the sobbing boy cried, "b . . . but if I had not l . . . l . . . lost the other one I w . . . would now have two."

Mr. De Wit and Afke laughed and left the little silly to this new grief.

In the meantime Tjerk had finished his errand and they all went on their way, passing a building which, judging by its high regular windows, seemed to be a school. They had guessed rightly, for a bell rang and the pupils poured out noisily for recess. When they saw our friends they cried, "Hullo, strangers!" and started throwing snowballs at them.

Of course the Elst children revenged themselves, and so it became a regular fight, even Teacher and Mr. De Wit joining.

You should have seen the pandemonium! Balls flew right, left, and center, high and low, some big and loose, some small and hard, hitting legs, backs, cheeks, and noses, bursting against window-panes or roofs and shedding their silver powder on everyone. Then there were screams and war cries of "Hurrah for Snaek!", "Hurrah for Elst!", and the rustling of skirts and starchy aprons as the girls bent to gather snow. Neither party would give in, and if the bell had not rung again, calling back the Snaek children to their class-rooms the fight might have continued till spring. But as it was, the enemy withdrew reluctantly after a few parting shots, leaving the Elst children masters of the field.

The Elst warriors now mopped their glowing faces and arranged their disheveled clothes, looking round to see whether there had been any casualties. No, the only serious case was that of Mr. De Wit, who hopped about frantically, twisting himself into all sorts of contortions, because a snowball had gone inside his collar and was now slowly trickling down his spine.

"Well, well," said Teacher, brushing the snow from his clothes, "that was a great battle. And the girls stuck it out beautifully. But I'm afraid it is getting time for us to turn back."

"He!" cried the children not at all keen to go home.

They walked back to the marketsquare and Teacher compared the time of his watch with the clock on the tower.

"Let's just have a look inside the church," said Mr. De Wit. "I believe they allow visitors."

"All right," agreed Teacher; "that won't take us long."

Mr. De Wit knocked at the door of a little house beside the church and an old man appeared with a large key in his hand.

"That's the sexton," whispered Jan to Okke.

Evert now thumped them excitedly on the shoulder. "That's great. He's going to open the door for us. This is our first real exploration. We must stick together."

They entered the spacious interior with the big whitewashed pillars supporting the vaulted roof. It was veiled in a mysterious darkness except for the streaks of sunlight which sifted through the high windows, scattering golden patterns over everything. Some scaffolding at the end showed that parts of the church were in repair, and the muffled sound of hammering told them that workmen were busy.

Teacher and Mr. De Wit were soon talking with the sexton, who showed them all the bits of carving on pews and pulpit, while the children roamed about, counting the big gray slabs on the floor and reading the inscriptions on tombs.

But Evert and his two friends walked away from the others. "It's a great chance. Surely we must do some exploring here," he whispered.

"Will we have time?" Okke asked, anxiously glancing at Teacher.

"It won't take long, and think! we might find a secret passage."

The three boys cautiously crept away toward a small door they had noticed and which was hidden from Teacher by some projecting piece of scaffolding. Jan opened it and the three boys disappeared, shutting the door quietly behind them.

But some one had seen them, all the same. Simon had been hovering near for some time, anxious to know their secret. Now he was standing before the little door through which the three had disappeared. He looked around. No one was near. Suddenly he thought he would follow the others. Why not? He opened the door and sniffed the musty smell of a stone passage. His curiosity was aroused and he went in.

Farther along, the passage ended in a dusty winding staircase which he began to climb and which seemed to lead up to the tower. The walls were damp and dark and the air got colder as he went higher. He held his breath and listened. Some little pebbles rolled down the stairs with a rattling noise. Then above his head he heard the sound of muffled laughter. He continued

That sent the others into a fresh volley of laughter. Simon struggled again, but not so forcibly. It began to dawn on him that they were playing some game. So he said, soberly, "Pansho, King of the Gypsies, asks why you have taken him captive."

Evert, too, became serious immediately. Drawing himself up full length, he replied: "The head of the Three Columbians would have you know that you have strayed into territory which belongs to them and therefore they will keep you till you swear you will not betray them."

"I swear!" Simon said, solemnly, happy that at last he had something to say.

"Then take off his bonds!" Evert commanded, graciously. Okke and Jan untied the handkerchiefs.

up, looking curiously about him, and came at last to a round wooden platform halfway up the staircase where a little window looked out on the square.

Suddenly he felt himself held by strong arms and three gruff voices said, "You're our prisoner!" Simon struggled and his eyes rolled wildly, but to his relief the ruffians were only Evert, Okke, and Jan.

"He! Let me go!" he cried. "What do you mean?"

But they bound his hands with a couple of grimy handkerchiefs and roared laughing. "He's our man Friday," Evert announced pompously.

"Or Winnetoo, the chief of the Indians," suggested Jan.

"Or Black Skull, captain of Pirates," added Okke.

Simon did not understand a word of this. "What do you mean?" he repeated. "I am nothing of the sort."

Suddenly *thump . . . thump!* they heard the sound of men's footsteps on the stairs above them.

"People!" whispered Evert. "Go down as quickly as you can." They tiptoed silently and swiftly down the winding steps, with the tramp of heavy boots behind them. Once back in the passage, they crouched behind an old discarded pew and waited breathlessly. The steps grew louder and a workman in blue overalls passed them without suspicion, his tool-box tucked under his arm.

When he had gone the boys crawled out of their hiding-place. The dust which lay as a thick gray carpet on the stone flags now clung to their trousers and hands. Even their faces were smeared.

"Good for you, Simon," the others cried. "You did not betray us."

Simon was thoroughly in the game. "Pansho never betrays anyone!"

Suddenly Jan started. "Look here. I am sure it's time to go back." Now they felt frightened and rushed to the little door, but when they turned the knob it wouldn't open. They looked stupidly at one another.

"Let me try," begged Simon. The others watched his futile efforts.

"I know what happened," Evert exclaimed. "That man has locked it."

Of course that was the explanation, but now what was to be done?

Jan and Okke kicked against the panel of the door and let out a cry for help which echoed through the passage, but there was no sign of anyone coming to their rescue, though they

listened for a long time. "This is terrible," groaned Jan, and Okke and Evert looked equally glum. But Simon, usually so depressed, kept up their spirits.

"Don't worry; we'll find a way out," he said, cheerfully. The others raised their heads with renewed hope.

"How? Where?"

"Well, we'll have to look for one," he answered.

"Of course," the others cried. "Aren't we silly? There are sure to be other doors." So the four boys went a-roaming through the dark passage.

In the meantime there was great consternation in the church. When it was time to go, Teacher had summoned his class and was surprised to find four of the boys missing. "Good gracious!

31

Where can they be?" he exclaimed. Then he added: "But we needn't worry. It is merely a joke, I am sure, and they are hiding somewhere."

This was the sign for a general search. They looked behind pillars and pews, in nooks and corners, the old grumbling sexton joining the search. But no boys were to be found.

"Now that's strange," Teacher said, with a puzzled frown. "What can have happened to them?"

"Look, there's a man coming out of a little door," cried Afke. "Perhaps he knows."

They saw the workman in the blue overalls shutting the door behind him and locking it with a key. Afke approached him timidly and inquired whether he had seen any boys.

"Boys?" the man asked, in great surprise. "What boys?"

"We have lost four of our party and we thought they might have gone through this door. . . ."

"Impossible!" said the man. "I would have seen them." He lifted his cap as Teacher approached him.

"You didn't see four boys?"

"No, sir, and it is not likely that they'd have escaped me if they had been there. I'd have taught them not to go traipsing around where they have no business to be." He seemed a surly, unpleasant kind of man and Teacher shrugged his shoulders.

"Ah, well."

"Look here," suggested Mr. De Wit, "can't they have gone outside? They may have got impatient and perhaps sneaked out when we weren't looking."

"The very thing!" Teacher cried, brightening visibly. "And they are waiting for us in the square."

They all trooped out, and the workman straightened his cap, shifted his quid, took up his box of tools, and went home. That's why there was no one to hear the thumps and cries of the boys when they found out that the door was locked.

Outside in the marketplace the late afternoon sun was tinting the snow on the roofs and casting long violet shadows on the ground. People were hurrying to and fro on errands, children played under the trees, and a dog barked, but the boys were nowhere to be seen. Teacher anxiously looked right and left, and Afke frantically collared an old gentleman, saying, breathlessly, "Did you see four boys, sir? We've lost four of our boys and one of them is my twin brother."

The gentleman was full of sympathy, "Dear, dear!" he muttered. "Dear, dear! No, I didn't see anyone, little maid. Tut, tut! This is too bad!" And he looked around reproachfully, as if blaming the whole world for this mishap. As usual in small towns, a crowd collected quickly, and Afke's tears caused quite a sensation. Messenger boys, servants, mothers with children, all gathered round the little group.

Teacher rushed into the church again, dreadfully worried. "What am I to do?" he cried, "What am I to do? Evert! . . . Okke! . . . Jan! . . . Simon!" But he heard no answering shout. He looked again in every conceivable place and even tried the little door, but it was locked, and, after all, the man had assured him that the boys could not have gone in there. He stroked his head with a trembling hand, imagining all sorts of terrible possibilities. Had the boys gone off without him? But surely they wouldn't do that. Simon, perhaps, but not Evert, not Jan, not Okke, no. What then could have happened? He rushed out again.

"The only thing we can do," he said to Mr. De Wit, "is to warn the police and ask them to look for them. We've done all we could, but, oh! what will their parents say?" he added, unhappily.

"Come, come," said Mr. De Wit, comforting him. "We may yet find them and, anyway, it is not likely that four strong boys will come to any harm." But he frowned and bit his lip. "Are you sure," he said, turning to the agitated little sexton, "that your church is not haunted?"

"Of course not," answered the sexton, indignantly.

It was a sad little procession that walked to the police office. Afke was inconsolable and many tears dropped on the snow as they went.

A stout constable took down notes. He wrote that Evert and Jan and Okke were fair, but that Simon was dark; that Simon was older and bigger than the others; and that Okke wore a bright red jersey. He often licked his pencil, and repeated the words slowly between little gasps as he jotted them down.

"Do you think," Teacher asked, "that you'll find them this evening?"

The constable settled his glasses straighter on his nose and looked very important. "All the necessary measures will be taken," he said, pompously, "but the result I cannot guarantee," and he plopped back into his chair again. When our friends left the cold bare office they felt more depressed than ever.

"What are we going to do?" Afke asked, lifting a tear-stained face.

Teacher gave her a pitying glance. "I don't know, lass, I don't know. I suppose we'll have to go without them. We cannot stay here all night."

"But we can't leave them," Afke cried, horror-stricken.

"What else can we do, child?"

They mournfully proceeded toward the canal, and when they had arrived there they gave one last despairing glance at the church. At that moment a wonderful thing happened.

Meanwhile the four boys had been looking for a way to escape from the tower. After a quarter of an hour's thorough search they were still unsuccessful, tired, and very disappointed. What, oh, what could they do? Poor Teacher! He would be so worried.

"Let's go up the stairs and have a look through the window," Simon suggested. Yes, of course, they might be able to see what was going on outside. They climbed up eagerly, their steps echoing against the stone walls. Jan looked pale and frightened.

"This is all your fault for bringing us here," he said, crossly, to Evert. "It was a ridiculous idea and my father will be furious. I'll never hear the end of it." And he groaned.

Evert defended himself. "If you thought it a stupid idea, why didn't you say so? Anyway, it was you yourself who proposed capturing Simon. Otherwise we might have been back in time."

"Look here, boys," said Okke, "if we are going to quarrel we

will never get out. We've got to pull ourselves together and think of something, or they will leave us here and then what will we do?" Evert and Jan stopped their quarreling, but Simon looked more worried than ever as he racked his brains for a solution.

Reaching the little platform again, they found the window so small that only one of them could look out at a time. Evert's turn was first.

"Such a crowd of people," he cried, pressing his nose to the glass. "What are they there for? Oh, I see Afke! She is crying, poor kid. Oh, what can we do about it?" and he turned away sadly.

"We must wave something or shout," proposed Simon. So they tried to open the window, but it was stuck fast.

Next, Jan had his peep through and let out a wail of consternation. "Look here, this is awful! They are leaving without us." Yes, the little procession was departing, slowly, reluctantly, but surely.

Okke and Evert sat down on the floor, staring at the toes of their boots with tear-dimmed eyes. They thought of the alarm their parents would feel when the party came home without them. They thought of a long cold night in that lonely tower without food or drink for hours to come, and never in their lives had they been so sad.

But Simon, having no one to grieve about, did not give up. "Look here, we must attract some one's attention," he said, sensibly. "It's foolish to think we're being left here when there are people all around us. Let's climb to the top of the tower and see if we can't get outside." The others meekly followed him as he suited the action to the word, glad that at least one of them was not discouraged.

The stairs ended in a platform from which doors and windows opened out on a circular balcony built for the benefit of visitors. They stepped outside and saw some more scaffolding at the back of the tower. This they supposed was where the man who had passed them had been working. They looked over the balustrade and saw people down below like little ants.

"Now make as much noise as you can," Simon said, and they started to wave their handkerchiefs, shouting for help, but the wind blew away the sounds and no one heard.

"Oh dear, it's no use!" Evert cried, leaning wearily against the wall and thrusting his hands in his pockets, for it was bitterly cold. The others shivered and suggested that they should go inside, which they sadly did.

"Where is Simon?" Jan asked in a moment. They looked around. Simon had disappeared.

"I suppose he gave up," said Okke, and rested his head in his hands. Jan sighed. They were the picture of misery as they stood there high above the snow-covered roofs, the last rays of the sun gilding their yellow heads.

And then the wonderful thing happened, as wonderful to them as to the little party out on the canal preparing to leave. For suddenly, shattering the peace of the departing day, a peal of church bells rang through the air. Not in the usual way, at the usual hour, but quite angrily, the notes tumbling over each other, clashing and wailing like lost children.

The three boys in the tower looked up, "Simon!" they cried. "To think we never thought of that." Their relief was so great that they made a kind of war dance, shouting, "Hurrah! Long live the king of the Gypsies!"

Yes, it was Simon. Wandering around, he had noticed the bell ropes and it had suddenly occurred to him to use them. But for this bright thought, I really don't know how the skating picnic would have ended. As it happened, people looked up curiously as soon as the discordant sounds rent the air, and hurried toward the square to see what the matter was.

Teacher also lifted his head and called out to the others: "Hark! That's not the usual way church bells ring." They listened for a moment. Then Teacher exclaimed in a tone of happy relief, "It's the boys! They're in the tower, after all, the rascals!" But he could not be angry, after all his anxiety.

35

"And . . . and . . . and . . . the man locked them up, after all. They were hiding so he didn't see them!" Afke cried, tumbling her words in eagerness. They took off their skates again and rushed toward the church. The sexton was already unlocking the doors.

"Those boys!" he grumbled, fumbling for the key of the little door inside. "They never seem to leave one a moment's peace."

But our class paid no attention; they were far too happy. The ringing of the bell stopped as soon as the sexton entered the church, and when he unlocked the little door four disheveled, dusty and eager boys leaped straight into Teacher's arms.

"Ho, ho! Easy a bit!" the victim of their onslaught exclaimed, but his relief was great.

Afke flung both arms round her brother's neck and held him tightly. "Oh, Evertje, Evertje! I thought I'd never see you again!" she cried.

"Get along with you!" Evert retorted, ashamed of such display. But the old sexton brushed away a tear of sympathy.

After the first excitement was over, Teacher spoke a few stern words to the culprits, but they were so sorry for what they had done that Teacher's heart softened and they did not get quite the scolding they deserved. Instead Mr. De Wit treated the whole party, including the sexton, to a cup of coffee each, at a neighboring restaurant, which warmed them up and seemed a fitting way to celebrate the return of the four prodigals.

"And now," Teacher said, when they had finished, "it is high time to go home." So they wiped their mouths and followed him to the canal, where they tied on their skates. Then Mr. De Wit shook hands with Teacher.

"I must leave you here," he said, regretfully, "but I'll come and visit you in Elst." Tjerk also had to return to his parents.

"Mind you tell your mother how grateful we are for her kindness," Teacher said to him, "and ask her to come and see us." Tjerk smiled, showing a row of white teeth.

"You must come back to us, some day," he urged, "all of you!"

After a parting shout our class pushed off, waving farewell to the two figures on the bank, which were soon swallowed up in the gathering gloom.

over everything. They had left the town far behind them and were cutting their way through fields in which a windmill, rising out of the dusk, looked like a black giant. They were all sleepy and shivery after their long day of air and exercise.

CHAPTER VI

Home Again

THE sun went down, leaving a golden streak on the horizon and some pink clouds. The brilliance of the snow faded and sharp outlines softened.

Evert, who still skated with his two friends, somewhat behind the others, invited Simon to join them. "We want to ask you something," he said, mysteriously.

Simon felt thrilled, "What is it?" he gladly answered.

"Well," Evert explained in hushed tones, "Jan and Okke and I have formed a club, a club of explorers, and we're going to build a hut at the back of our farm. It's a secret and we're not going to have any more members, except perhaps Afke once in a while. But you've been so splendid today with everything that we want you to come in with us." He looked eagerly at Simon.

Simon's eyes glittered and he squeezed Evert's hands as though he would crush them. "You're a brick, Evert. I've always wanted to be your friend."

"And I think," Evert said, musingly, "that I also wanted to be your friend."

They skated back arm in arm to the other two Columbians. "He's joining us," Evert cried, triumphantly.

By now the approaching night was casting its dark shadow

Teacher, too, felt tired. He was afraid that the children would not be home in time, and the party which had so cheerfully begun its journey that morning now drooped as though the sun had taken all its joy with it.

The wind rose and blew against them, freezing faces and hands into numbness and flapping the girls' skirts against their legs. It was impossible to sing, and they pulled along silently, too weary even to speak. Here and there, as the gray shadows deepened and the faint glow at the horizon faded away, twinkling lights appeared beckoning the children to comfortable homes not their own and making them long the more for Elst.

"Please, sir, can't we rest a bit?" Afke said at last, in a pitiful little voice.

Teacher looked anxiously at his watch. The adventure in the tower had taken up much time. It would soon be quite dark, and though it is possible to skate at night, it is not safe to do so. He frowned, yet when they all said they were too tired to go on, he had to allow them a moment's pause.

So they sat for a while on a little wooden gate, looking at the vast expanse of dark sky that stretched above them, longing for the comfort of their warm beds. Alas! First they must skate a long way on their aching feet.

But as though a fairy had heard their secret wish, a cheerful sound suddenly broke the silence—the jingling of merry little bells and the clattering of horses' hooves on the ice. The boys jumped up and gave a wild cheer as a big sledge drawn by magnificent white horses emerged like a ghost out of the night.

The sledge was empty and with a cry of delight Teacher hailed the driver. "Can you give us a lift?"

"Where to?"

"To Elst."

"Righto. I'm going there myself. Hop in, everybody," said the man.

Such luck! The girls scrambled into the sledge, where they immediately snuggled underneath the rugs, and the boys tied their pole to the sledge so that they could be dragged along behind. The girls, who had been miserable a moment before, felt a delicious warmth stealing through their bodies. They gazed up happily at the sky where stars began to appear and twinkle down on them. Gradually the steady click-clack of the horses' hooves and the rhythmic jingling of the bells soothed them to sleep. But Teacher and the boys, kept well awake by the icy wind, started to sing the Dutch version of "Twinkle, Twinkle, Little Star," and so the skating picnic became a triumphant procession which at last landed in Elst.

Teacher helped the girls out, for they were very stiff and scarcely able to stand on their swollen feet. The driver would not hear of thanks.

38

"No, not at all; it was a pleasure," he said. He touched his cap, clicked his tongue, and the horses went off at a brisk trot, all the little bells tinkling their good-by. He was soon swallowed up in the darkness.

Now sixteen hands were offered to Teacher, and sixteen mouths murmured, "Thank you for the lovely day, sir."

He pulled Evert aside, saying, "Tell your mother that I'll come and explain about the accident as soon as possible." He patted the boy's head and departed, some of the children escorting him home, carrying the pole for him. The others left after cheerful good-bys.

Evert especially grasped Simon's hand, "Cheerio, gypsy! See you tomorrow. I think we'll keep on calling you Pansho. It suits you. And don't forget that you're a Columbian now. We must have an opening celebration of the club soon, but mind it's a secret. So long!"

Simon nodded and promised and waved and went home happier than he had ever thought he could be. His loneliness was over. He had friends, and especially one friend, of whom he felt proud. Now his uncle could no longer grumble at his timidity. He would be like other boys. The thought made his feet dance over the snow and his heart sing with gratitude.

Afke and Evert walked home silently. They were cold and tired and hungry, but when they came within sight of home they hurried along. Mother received them with her affectionate smile and kissed their glowing cheeks. The lamp shed its yellow light on the old familiar objects and their dinner stood simmering on the stove. They took off their wraps and shoes and stockings.

Suddenly Mother blinked her eyes in amazement. "Evert, you've got different clothes on," she cried. Yes, that was true; the twins had forgotten all about it. So they told the story of the accident as well as they could while eating their dinner, and Mother was deeply shocked.

"My dear!" she cried, throwing up her hands. "You might have been drowned!" The children were rather proud of Mother's excitement, especially as she at once rushed outside to call Father, to whom the story had to be told all over again. The parents shook their heads gravely and Father put his hand on Evert's forehead to see if he had fever.

"Ah, the lad's all right," he said, relieved and rather proud of his strong son. "He's never been ill in his life and he's not going to start now. Don't worry, Mother."

Mother looked carefully at Evert. "Yes, he does seem all right," she admitted. "Well, and what else happened?"

Now the twins told the adventure of the tower, Evert describing what happened inside, and Afke what happened outside, and their father and mother listened quite spellbound.

"Well, you have had a time of it, I must say," they exclaimed, and they praised Simon gratefully. For the twins had taken care to forget nothing and had described Simon's behavior in such a way that, had the boy been there, he would have blushed to the roots of his hair.

The twins finished their dinner and Evert went over to his father and leaned against his knees. "Daddy," he said, looking coaxingly into his father's eyes.

"What, my lad?"

"I want to ask you a favor."

"Ask away and if it is in my power I shall grant it to you," Father said, looking affectionately into his son's eager face.

"I want the little patch of barren land at the back of the farm for my very own. I and my friends have a secret and we need some place where no one else can come. May I?"

"Dear me!" said Father. "And am I to hear nothing of the secret?"

Evert shook his head. "No, but it is not a wicked one," he said.

"All right, boy, I trust you. But I gave you the land some time ago, didn't I? You may do with it whatever you like."

Here Afke chimed in, indignantly, "Evert, are you going to have a place where I mayn't come?"

"Perhaps," Evert said mysteriously, "perhaps, you may join us. But I must first consult the others," for he now had an idea about Afke and the Columbians. Explorers often took women

helpers to cook their food, now, didn't they? Yes, Afke could be the Columbians' cook!

Evert kissed his father good night, for he was very tired. Then he flung his arms round his mother's neck and whispered, "Mother, I want to have a little party soon for three of my friends, and I want you to make a nice cake."

"All right, my boy, you shall have one. I'm so glad to have you back," murmured Mother.

"We're glad to be back, too," said Afke, kissing her.

Mother now lit a candle and saw the twins to bed, tucking the bedclothes firmly around them and gazing at them fondly as they closed their eyes. Then she tiptoed out, leaving the little room dark but for the little night light flickering on the table. Night crept on with silver feet. The wise and distant moon pushed her full face through the clouds, shedding an eerie light on the snowy roofs. One by one the window lights popped out. The village slept.

THE END

Help with Pronunciation

(phrases in quotation marks are from the author)

Consonants

J   is pronounced as Y:

Jan	Yahn
Sjollemah	Syoh le mah
Tjerk	Tyurk (yu as in *museum*)
Siepertje	See pert yuh
Poffertjes	Poh fert yus

V   is sometimes pronounced as F, as in Van:

Wilhelmus Van Nassaue   Wilhelmus *Fahn* Nassowe
(aue as in *ow*)

. . . but other times, remains V, as in Evert:

Evert (E is like *a* in *say*; second e is unstressed *e* as in *the*)

G and CH are both pronounced between English *ch* and *k:*
"like a G, sharp in the throat"

Baanveger	Bahn fay chur
Och	"like the Gaelic och"
Och die arme yongen	Okh dee armuh yong uhn
Michiel de Ruyter	Meecheel duh Ruyter
	(Ruy rhymes with English *guy*)

Vowels

Afke	*a* as in *far; e* as in *the:* Ahfkuh
Arie	Ahree
Kraam	open your mouth even further than in *far*: Kraahm
Korstje	"*o* as in *hot*": Kors yuh
Okke	"*o* as in *short*": Ohk kuh
Leeuwarden	Lay war (as in *bar*) den
Friesland	Freez lahnd
Frisian	Freez ee uhn
Zuyder Zee	Zider (as in *cider*) Zay
Ryksmuseum	*i* as in *bike*: Riks museum
Winterkoninkje	English *Winter;* Winter koh nink yuh
Dank ye vel	Dahnk yuh vel